A Halloween Mystery

A Halloween Mystery

Who?

What?

Why?

by Addy H.

illustrated by
Edgar Larrazabal

ISBN: 1508794618

ISBN 13: 9781508794615

Library of Congress Control Number: 2015904419

CreateSpace Independent Publishing Platform, North Charleston, SC

On a dark, misty night when the moon was dim and gloomy, Mr. Owl was flying by the Old River Road. He could not believe his eyes!

Mr. Owl saw thirteen witches hanging upside down. The witches were hanging on an enormous tree.

"Oh, my!" gasped Mr. Owl. *Can this be thirteen witches hanging upside down?* he thought.

Mr. Owl flew toward the witches and asked, "Hello? Hello down there. Is everything OK?"

The witches did not answer.

"Hm," said Mr. Owl as he returned to his tree. He scratched his head and said, "This is not right. I'd better fly to the Halloween party downtown and ask if anyone knows about the witches hanging upside down."

Mr. Owl flew so fast that he almost got a ticket from the police officer who was directing traffic.

Mr. Owl arrived at the Halloween party. Every Halloween creature he could think of was there.

Mr. Owl spotted Werewolf, Dracula, and Frankenstein all standing together, so he flew over to them and said, "Am I glad to see you."

"Something strange is happening on the Old River Road," Mr. Owl said. "Thirteen witches are hanging upside down on an enormous tree."

Werewolf turned around and howled.

Then he replied, "Oh my! That is interesting. Did you ask the witches why they were hanging upside down?"

"Yes; yes, I did," Mr. Owl said. "But they did not answer."

"Hm," said Werewolf.

Dracula and Frankenstein shook their heads and said, "My, my, that is strange."

Then Dracula said, "Let's all go to the Old River Road," and off they went.

When they arrived, the witches were still hanging upside down.

Werewolf said, "I know! I will howl and howl at the moon, and that should make them talk."

"That sounds like a good idea," replied Dracula, Frankenstein, and Mr. Owl in unison.

Werewolf got on his haunches and howled at the moon, but nothing happened. Then he howled and howled again and again, and still nothing happened.

The witches did not move.

Dracula said, "Move over! I, Dracula, will find out what is going on." He opened up his cape, his eyes turned red, and a strong wind blew. "Come; come to me, and look into my eyes!"

But the witches did not move.

Again, Dracula shouted, "Come; come to me and look into my eyes!" but nothing happened.

Frankenstein pushed Dracula to the side and said, "Move over! I, Frankenstein, will get the witches to tell us why they are hanging upside down."

Frankenstein started to stomp on the ground. He was such a big man and he stomped so hard that the tree started to dance. Soon, he was dancing the "Monster Mash."

It looked like so much fun that Dracula and Werewolf also started dancing the "Monster Mash."

The trees were really moving, and the witches were swinging every which way. "Stop! Stop!" yelled one of the witches. "What are you doing?"

Dracula shouted back, "Vat? Vat? Vat are we doing? You're the thirteen silly witches who are hanging upside down and who are not talking or answering our questions."

"OK, OK!" replied one of the witches.

"We are waiting for a bright, full moon," the witch said. "That is when our brooms come to life."

Just as the witch was about to continue talking, the full moon became so bright that it lit up the dark, misty, and gloomy night.

As the witches' brooms came out of nowhere, Mr. Owl yelled, "Watch out down there!"

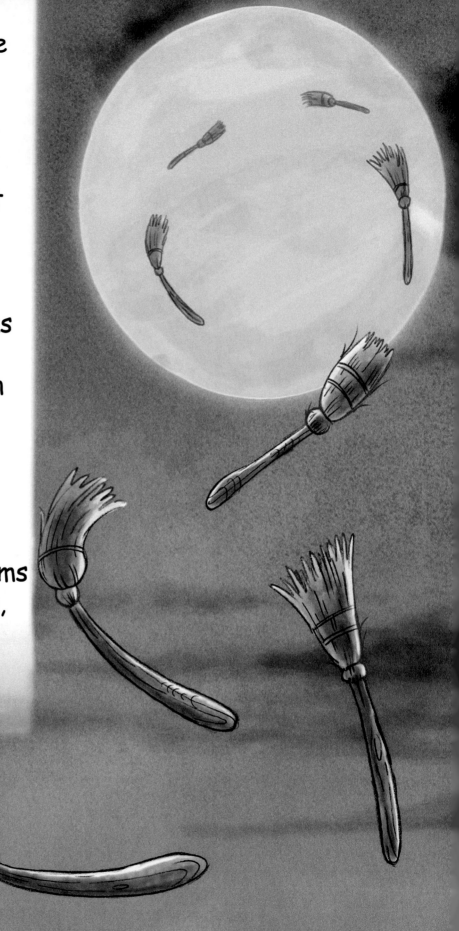

The witches got on their brooms and circled around
Mr. Owl, Werewolf, Dracula, and Frankenstein.
The witches shouted, "Didn't you hear about the big
Halloween party happening downtown? They are giving
out candies, cookies, and gum galore with contests and
prizes and much more!"

All the witches yelled, "Happy Halloween!" as they
flew into the night.

Yes. It was a strange sight to see thirteen whimsical witches flying upside down blowing bubbles.

Halloween Quiz

1. Why were the witches hanging upside down? And when they flew into the night, why did they also fly upside down?
2. Why weren't the witches able to speak when Mr. Owl asked them a question?
3. What is the significance of thirteen witches?

See next page for answers.

Answers

*   Below are possible answers to the questions. But you can have any answer you want because all answers are correct. So use your imagination and have fun sharing your creative answers with others.

1.   The witches were hanging upside down because they are silly witches and thought they had to be upside down because the Halloween party was happening *down*town.

2.   The reason the witches could not speak to Mr. Owl was because their mouths were full of chewing gum, and they were practicing for the bubblegum contest.

3.   The significance of thirteen witches is that when the number 13 is reversed, it becomes 31, the day of Halloween.

Addy H. has been writing for 30 years. Most of her work consists of nonfiction children's stories. Her inspiration for these stories came from raising her own six children. On her free time, Addy H. enjoys spending time with her grandchildren, playing bingo, and reading mystery novels.

Visit Addy H. at Addyh.com and Like her on Facebook

Made in the USA
Middletown, DE
28 September 2015